MW00916349

# Princess Ballerinas

# The Nutcracker

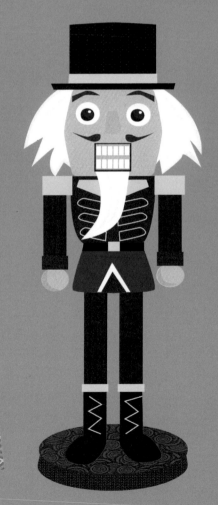

Created and Written by Megan Meyers
Edited and Illustrated by Joanna Jarc Robinson

This book is dedicated to YOU!
May you enjoy a lifetime of
dancing, music, and letting your
imagination soar!

It was almost Christmas! Miss Megan had a surprise for her class. She had decorated the dance studio with twinkling lights and a small Christmas tree. Three smiling Princess Ballerinas danced in to the room with extra excitement.

Once in their meeting circle, Miss Megan said, "Hello, girls. Today we are going to learn about a Christmas ballet called *The Nutcracker*. You will need to imagine what we see and do. Let's get ready. Close your eyes and repeat after me..."

**If I close my eyes and put my mind to it,**
**I can imagine! There's nothing to it!**

The girls closed their eyes and said the magic words.
When they opened their eyes...

They imagined an amazing holiday display! There was a tall Christmas tree covered with bright, twinkling lights, and ornaments in every color. Everything was just beautiful!

ofia noticed lots of presents under the tree – each one was wrapped perfectly.
Isabella imagined four stockings hanging from the mantle.
Mia saw milk and cookies on the table for Santa. "It's Christmas Eve," she said.

"That's right," said Miss Megan, "*The Nutcracker* story begins on Christmas Eve at the home of Clara and her brother, Fritz. Their family is having a party. One of the guests is their godfather, Drosselmeyer. He is a toymaker and he has a special gift for the children."

"What is it? What is it?" asked Mia excitedly.
"I bet it's a doll," guessed Isabella. "I think it's a game," said Sofia.
"Good ideas," said Miss Megan, "but the gift is was a nutcracker that Drosselmeyer made, and some toy soldiers." The Princess Ballerinas looked confused. They had never seen a nutcracker before. Luckily, Miss Megan had one to show them. She explained how it could be used to crack nuts, like walnuts or pecans. She showed them how it moved.
Its arms and legs were stiff and straight.

The girls walked around the room with stiff arms and legs like the nutcracker.

Sofia moved her jaw up and down, just like the nutcracker. She looked so silly.

Miss Megan continued the story, "Unfortunately, Fritz was careless with the nutcracker and he broke it. Clara was very sad. She fell asleep near the Christmas tree with the nutcracker by her side. Then she had strange and magical dream..."

"The nutcracker and the toy soldiers came to life! They fought an army of mice, including a mouse with 7 heads!" Miss Megan told them.

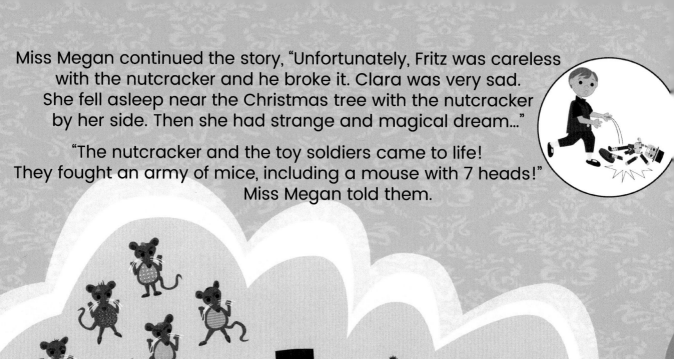

Then the Princess Ballerinas performed leaps and turns like the nutcracker and the toy soldiers.

They pretended they were fighting the mice, too.

"The nutcracker turned into a Prince," said Miss Megan.

"He took Clara to the Land of Snow."

The Princess Ballerinas danced like snowflakes!

They jumped.
They spun in circles and twirled around the dance floor.

"Beautiful snowflakes!" exclaimed Miss Megan.

"What happens after the Land of Snow?" wondered Mia.

"Well," said Miss Megan, "the Prince took Clara to the Land of Sweets where they met the Sugarplum Fairy."

The Princess Ballerinas cheered, "Yay! A fairy!"

Miss Megan said, "The Prince and Clara watched several sweet andspecial dances. We will try them all!"

First, they did the dance of the Sugarplum Fairy. They were light on their feet with graceful arm movements called port de bras.

Next, they practiced the Spanish Chocolate Dance. They made large, sweeping movements with their arms and legs.

Then they did the Arabian Coffee Dance. That one had slow, careful movements like arabesque.

After that, they did the Chinese Tea dance, which included quick hops and jumps called sautés.

After a quick water break, they continued with the Russian Candy Cane Dance. They pretended to be candy canes with straight arms and legs as they balanced in relevé.

Finally, they tried the French Marzipan Mirliton Dance. The girls danced together, performing each of the dances in the Land of Sweets.

Miss Megan explained that in the ballet, a character named Mother Ginger has her children run out from under her giant skirt to perform for the Prince and Clara.

The Princess Ballerinas thought that was a very silly idea.

The last dance Miss Megan showed them was the Waltz of the Flowers.
They crouched down near the ground, pretending they were budding seeds.
Then they slowly moved their bodies and grew into tall, beautiful flowers.

They danced gracefully
around the room.

Miss Megan called the dancers to the circle. She turned off the room lights and turned on the Christmas lights. They twinkled and sparkled! They were so beautiful! "What did you learn today?" she asked the Princess Ballerinas.

Mia said, "I learned how to do the Spanish Chocolate dance, the Chinese Tea dance, and a waltz."

Isabella said, "I learned how to dance like a flower and a snowflake, and a soldier, and even a candy cane!"

Sofia said, "I learned that a nutcracker can crack nuts, and can fight an army of mice. Hi-yah! Everyone laughed.

Then Miss Megan gave each Princess Ballerina a sweet, little surprise and wished them a Merry Christmas. "Thank you! Merry Christmas!" shouted the Princess Ballerinas. Then they twirled out the door to meet their parents.

Princess Ballerinas

Make your own nutcracker ornament!
What you will need:

empty toilet paper roll    glue    scissors    string or ribbon    hole punch

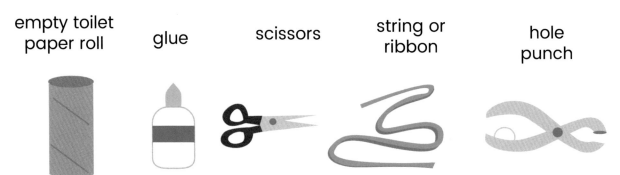

What to do:
1. Cut out the nutcracker along the dotted line.
2. Put glue on the toilet paper roll.
3. Wrap the nutcracker paper around the toilet paper roll.
4. Ask an adult to help punch a hole through the red dots.
5. Poke your string through one hole, then the other.
6. Tie a bow with the ends of the string.
7. Hang the ornament on your Christmas tree!

What gift would you like to receive?
Draw a picture of something on your Christmas list.

Color the nutcracker.

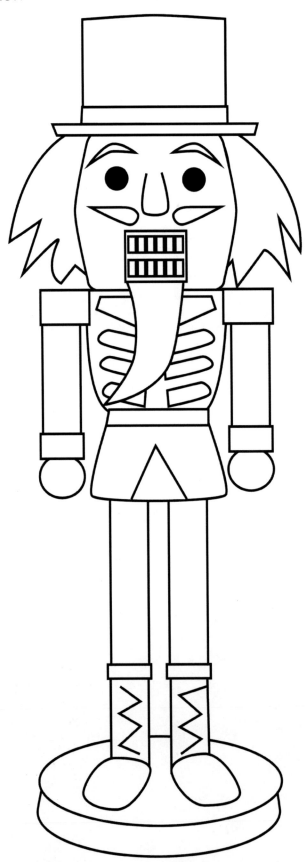

## About Princess Ballerinas

The Princess Ballerinas dance program is a <u>REAL</u> dance program created <u>JUST</u> for little ballerinas like Sofia, Mia, Isabella, and your child, too!

Our passion is to inspire joy in children by providing a truly magical experience using the power of story, imagination, music, and dance.

To find a Princess Ballerinas class near you, please visit:
www.PrincessBallerinas.com

16109652R00015

Made in the USA
Middletown, DE
25 November 2018